A HOME TO HAUNT

Sudeshna Shome Ghosh

Illustrations by Pankaj Saikia

HARPERCOLLINS
CHILDREN'S BOOKS

First published in India by HarperCollins *Children's Books* 2025
An imprint of HarperCollins *Publishers*
HarperCollins *Publishers* India, Cyber City, Building 10-A, Gurugram, Haryana-122002, India
www.harpercollins.co.in

2 4 6 8 10 9 7 5 3 1

Text © Sudeshna Shome Ghosh 2025
Illustrations © HarperCollins *Publishers* India 2025

P-ISBN: 978-93-6989-654-7
E-ISBN: 978-93-6989-521-2

Sudeshna Shome Ghosh asserts the moral right
to be identified as the author of this work.

This is a work of fiction and all characters and incidents described
in this book are the product of the author's imagination.
Any resemblance to actual persons, living or dead, is entirely coincidental.

All rights reserved. No part of this publication may be reproduced,
stored in a retrieval system, or transmitted, in any form or by any means,
electronic, mechanical, photocopying, recording or otherwise, without
the prior permission of the publishers.

Without limiting the exclusive rights of any author, contributor or the
publisher of this publication, any unauthorized use of this publication
to train generative artificial intelligence (AI) technologies is expressly
prohibited. HarperCollins also exercise their rights under Article 4(3) of
the Digital Single Market Directive 2019/790 and expressly reserve this
publication from the text and data-mining exception.

Illustrations: Pankaj Saikia
Cover design: Pankaj Saikia

Typeset in 12/18 Bembo Std at
HarperCollins *Publishers* India

Printed and bound at
Thomson Press (India) Ltd.

This book is produced from independently certified FSC® paper
to ensure responsible forest management.

HarperCollins *Publishers*, Macken House, 39/40 Mayor Street Upper,
Dublin 1, D01 C9W8, Ireland

To Rana and Opu

1

Everything changed the day Mama and I set off for Jalpaiguri by the Darjeeling Mail. I had been looking forward to going there for ages. I had a whole month's holiday for Durga Puja, and I wanted to spend it with my cousins Bulti and Pencha.

I had packed three Amar Chitra Kathas, the new fat Percy Jackson, my favourite Feluda book, and umpteen other storybooks and comics in my bag, and the Ludo set I got for my birthday. My cousins have a Ludo set, but mine also has Snakes and Ladders on the other side. Pencha can play Ludo for hours. He can also eat as many guavas as you give him. Once he ate fifteen. He had a tummy ache after.

My cousins were going to come from Delhi with my aunt, while I was going from Kolkata. This was how we spent all our school holidays—at our grandparents' home in Siliguri. But this time my uncle was taking me there. It was going to be one whole month of playing hide-and-seek in the large garden with the big old trees, chasing the hens around the hen house, and petting Tengri the dog, who visited us whenever he felt like it.

Ma had checked my bag and, shaking her head, added some clothes with the books I'd stuffed in. So anyway, my bag was packed and ready, and I was all set to leave for Sealdah station by 7 p.m. The train left at 10 p.m., but there were always traffic jams on the roads of Kolkata. Once, we had to run down Howrah Bridge, our bags, clothes and shoes all flying behind us as we rushed to catch the Rajdhani Express. I felt quite silly doing that.

The problem was, there was no sign of Mama.

'Babu!' Ma yelled to her brother, who had been sitting in the bathroom for one hour.

'Mama!' I added to the chorus.

'Coming!' Mama yelled back.

The door of the bathroom was flung open and Mama rushed out in a flurry of aftershave and soap and talcum powder.

'Poltu? Ready?' he asked me in a loud voice.

Ready? I was more ready than Phantom when the drums start playing in the jungle.

We picked up our bags and, after a last round of goodbyes to Ma, jumped into the waiting taxi.

'See he does not eat too much rubbish,' Ma called out a final set of instructions. 'And remember your holiday homework too … '

'Yes, Ma. Bye bye! See you soon.'

I waved to Ma till we reached the end of the lane. Then, as we took the turn at the phuchka stall, I settled back into the squeaky, half-torn taxi seat and rubbed the wetness of her kisses from my cheeks.

Mama was looking at me, his eyes twinkling.

'So, Shriman Palash Ranjan Sen, urf Poltu, are you ready?'

I gave him a quick look from the corner of my eye. 'Ready for what? To run down the platform to catch our train?'

'Relax, there's plenty of time. The train to Jalpaiguri is at least two hours late every day. Once we reach the station, I will treat you to a Thums Up, okay?'

I nodded. Ma rarely allowed me to have cold drinks, more so before a train ride (that meant extra trips to the bathroom). But I was now 8.5 years old and this was my first trip without her.

I was all ready to lead the life of an adventurer!

2

As the taxi stopped and started and wheezed its way through Kolkata, I craned my head to catch as much as I could see out of the window. The city looked so different during the night. There were lights everywhere. So many people were walking on the streets, some rushing, some just standing and chatting. Many were eating their dinner sitting on benches at roadside stalls. When our taxi stopped for what seemed like an hour next to one such stall, I watched the men and women there eating ruti and torkari being served by a young boy, as a grumpy-looking lady sat behind a stove churning out one ruti after another. A white cat smacked its lips next to her, waiting for some stray bits of food.

Mama seemed to have sunk into his thoughts and was staring at the night sky with an absent look in his eyes. 'You know, Poltu,' he said suddenly, 'right now, to the right of us are 2000 tombs and graves. Imagine, we are sitting in a traffic jam here, but unknown to us, there are around 2000 ghosts and ghouls floating around on the other side of that wall.'

He pointed to a wall that ran down the side of the road. I turned my neck to see. There were some tall trees standing behind the wall, and no lights at all.

'What is that place, Mama?' I asked.

'South Park Street Cemetery. Do you remember reading about it? The first Europeans who came to Kolkata are buried there. In those days many of these Englishmen, women, and children died for various reasons—illness, the heat, duels …'

'What are duels?'

'A duel was a fight between two people. One would challenge the other, and they would meet somewhere in the open, along with a partner each. Then they had one chance to shoot or attack each other with swords or some other weapon. The one who was left standing won.'

Mama and I stared out of the window as the taxi picked up speed. I had read about the cemetery in books.

I was seeing it for the first time. I kept looking out of the back window till the trees faded away in the evening traffic. Were there really 2000 ghosts floating around there? Why would ghosts live in cities? Didn't they prefer quieter, darker places so they could haunt in peace?

My friend Nimai claims to have met a ghost once. The ghost was walking down our paara and stopped to ask Nimai the time. None of us wore a watch, and neither did Nimai. Just as he was about to say he didn't know the time, he heard the evening conch shell, which was blown every evening at 6 o'clock at Binti's house by her Dida, and, in front of his eyes, the man slowly evaporated.

'He just became smoke!' Nimai told us later.

None of us believed him then. Why would a bhoot come to our paara and want to know the time? And then why would he just vanish like smoke without waiting to hear the answer? It made no sense.

But now, as I sat back in the taxi and thought of all those long-dead men and women buried right in the middle of the city, I had to wonder. My city was much larger and stranger than I'd ever thought. What secrets did it have that I didn't know about?

3

We finally reached Sealdah station at 9 o'clock. The huge clock on the station wall told the time. As soon as we got off the taxi, we were surrounded by many men in red, asking us if we wanted them to carry our suitcases. But Mama and I were only carrying one small bag each, so we didn't need any help. All the other times I'd been to the station, Ma had hired a coolie. This one time, I could not believe how many items the man had strung up all over his body. Two large suitcases on his head, one bag on his shoulder, and another small bag on the other shoulder! Then he sped off so fast towards the platform that Ma sent me running after him, to keep an eye on our luggage. I thought being a porter was quite a neat job. Imagine being able to carry so many heavy bags at one time, like a superhero! But then later

I saw Ma pay the man fifty rupees and he went and joined some of his friends who were drinking tea and eating small, sweet buns. They all looked very tired.

So I was happy that I could carry my own bag this time. Mama quickly checked the display board to see where our train was supposed to come and if it was running late. It was indeed late, as he had predicted.

'Poltu, stay by me, okay?' Mama warned. There were so many people rushing around with huge bags, pushing and jostling, it would've been quite easy for us to lose one another.

I trotted close to Mama. There was a weird smell hanging in the air. It was the smell of smoke, sweat and food all rolled into each other. I sniffed hard. I thought it smelt of grown-up adventures.

Mama and I reached platform 11, from where our train was supposed to leave. We still had a good three hours to go. Mama spotted the edge of a bench that was empty and told me to sit on it. At other times, we just used our luggage as benches, but this time our small bags would not do.

'Where are you going?' I asked, as Mama set off as soon as I sat down, the two bags at my feet. There was a man sleeping on the bench, covered from head to toe in a scratchy old blanket. He was all curled up, so there was some space by his feet where I could sit.

'Thums Up!' was all Mama called out, before vanishing.

I sat there quietly, looking around me. I had read enough Feluda, Alex Rider and Famous Five stories to know that one always needed to observe one's surroundings carefully. Who knew what mysteries lay hidden all around! For example, this man, who was sleeping next to me—why was he sleeping right here in the middle of the noisy platform with so many people rushing all around him?

A little black dog came sniffing around my feet. I looked at it carefully. Was it a stray? Or was it a detective's sidekick, like Snowy?

'Poltu, take this.' I jumped at Mama's loud voice in my ear. While I had been sitting and observing, he had gone to the refreshment stall. He held a brand-new Phantom comic in his hand! And a packet of Gems! 'What? Are you happy now?' Mama grinned. I was so happy I could barely thank him. 'Arrey it's your first time away from your mother. You deserve a little gift from your Mama.'

As I took the comic and the Gems from him, his eye flickered to the man sleeping by me. Did I imagine it, or did Mama's expression become a little serious? But when I looked at him again, he was back to being my favourite uncle, the one who bought me 5 Star chocolates and told the best/worst knock-knock jokes.

'Won't you sit, Mama?' I asked.

'Umm, no. You keep the seat. Are you going to read the comic now? Okay good, good,' Mama said, a bit absent-mindedly. 'Poltu, keep an eye on the bags. I will be right back. Let me get the Thums Up.' Saying this, Mama disappeared again.

How odd! What was he up to? My Mama, or Shankar Das, is usually a fund of stories. He knows *everything*. He tells me about far-off places in India and outside, from Kashmir to Sri Lanka to Madagascar. He can do magic tricks. He can do huge sums very fast in his head. And best of all, none of us knows exactly what he does. Ma says he needs to get a job in an office. Whenever she says this, Mama laughs very hard. But if I ever ask him, 'Where did you go today, Mama? Office?' he just shakes his head, laughs some more, and produces an egg from my nose. Ma was not too happy about sending me to Siliguri alone with him, muttering that he was 'irresponsible'.

Mama has lived with us ever since I can remember. I know my father only from some photos in the house, but Mama has always been there. I had even gone to nursery school perched on his shoulder. But every few months, he disappears without a word. No one knows where he goes, or what he does. When he comes back from these mysterious trips, he is tired and sleeps almost all day. Then in some time, he goes back to being the fun, jokey, absent-minded uncle I love so much.

This time, Ma had no choice but to send me off with him. Her own study trip to Finland was coming up and she needed to prepare for it. My mother is a climate scientist, and next year, she's going to the Arctic Circle to study how the shrinking ice is affecting the polar bears. I have seen her reading reports with lots of numbers and graphs. They show how the ice is melting away fast, and the poor bears are not able to hunt like before. She needed this month to read and plan and study, so me going off to my grandparents' house with Mama was the best solution for her.

And that's how I ended up at Sealdah station, about to open the new Phantom comic. It had an exciting picture

of the 'Ghost Who Walks' on the cover, in his purple bodysuit, surrounded by his wolf and his horse, about to throw a punch at a villain. I opened the box of Gems and shook it till a red one popped up. I always eat a red one first. Then a blue, then a green.

The red Gems had almost leapt into my hand. Something sure was strange today! Usually, I really have to look for it. I put it into my mouth and stared at the open page on my lap.

Why were the pictures so hazy?

I could barely make out the words.

I brought the book closer to my eyes.

It was still hard to see.

Because ... everything had gone black.

All the lights in the station blinked off as if someone had blown out a candle in one giant breath.

All around me was silence and darkness.

4

Was it loadshedding? Did railway stations have power cuts? I gripped my book and felt for the bags at my feet. Ma had told me enough times to look out for bag snatchers. But something even stranger was happening. The air around me seemed to be shifting. A cool breeze prickled through my hair. Then it got stronger and stronger. I was sure a whirlwind was picking up speed around us.

Then it felt like a train was rolling into the station. But it was not coming in slowly, the way trains do when they reach a station. This train was rushing in. I could hear the thundering of its wheels, the creak of its doors and windows. My hands flew to my ears.

I didn't realize I had closed my eyes as well. When the rumble of the train died away, I slowly opened my eyes. The lights were still out. But there was a faint glow ... almost like moonlight. That was enough for me to see quite clearly all around me.

A train was standing on the rail line and there was a lot of smoke in the air because steam was billowing from the train's engine. I had never seen an actual steam engine on a train outside the movies. It was making loud wheezing, gushing sounds as it stood there. Some people were getting off the train—white and shadowy figures, or so it looked to me in that faint light.

'Mama,' I called out shakily. This was all too eerie. There was no sign of Mama. I looked around and then, I nearly jumped out of my skin in fright. Where the man in the blanket had been sleeping, there now sat an oldish man. He was dressed in old-style clothes—a dhoti and a kurta, and on his nose were thick glasses through which his eyes looked very large. He was staring right at me.

'Hnello, bnoy,' he mumbled in a nasal tone.

'H-hello,' I replied, not knowing what else to say.

After saying hello, the man seemed to sink into deep thought. But he kept looking at me. Or rather, he was looking at what I was holding in my hands. I was still clutching the packet of Gems.

The man was looking at it with a very sad expression on his face. Did he want one? He looked forlornly at the packet, and then at me, and then back at the packet. What was going on? What should I do? Of course, Ma had told me hundreds of times not to accept any food or drink from strangers. But what was I supposed to do if a stranger wanted food or drink from *me*? Or, as in this case, Gems?

'Do you want one?' I extended the packet towards the man.

A huge grin split his face. I mean, it actually broke his face into an upper and a lower part. His eyes hung in the air, and his mouth floated below them. In the middle, for a brief moment, there seemed to be air. I shut my eyes tight, counted to five quickly, and opened

them again. His face had closed up by then but the smile lingered.

He took the packet of Gems from my hand and shook it happily. He didn't look all that old and tired now. He rummaged around and took out one candy (I couldn't make out the colour in the dim light), then he popped it into his mouth and sighed.

Really, this was very odd. I had never seen a grown-up look so delighted eating Gems.

'Thnank ynou bnoy,' he said in that same nasal tone and returned the packet to me. I was able to see him even more clearly—he was getting put together from smoke into real skin and clothes.

There was such a look of joy on his face, it was as if I had given him a plate of mutton curry and rice. I opened my mouth to ask him if he wanted one more, but I froze. Right behind my neck I could feel a cold wind tickling—just like when I opened the fridge door on a summer night and let the cold wash over me. But this was a different cold. It was chilly. There was a ripple in the dark air all around me, and for the first time ever, I knew what books meant when they said 'hair prickling at the back of my neck'.

The man was looking at something behind me.

I turned around slowly, not sure if I really wanted to see what was there. But my head was moving on its own, like a puppet.

Three very thin men were standing behind me. They were all dressed similarly, like the other man, in old dhotis and kurtas. There was something smoky and wispy about them as well. The only thing that was bright were their eyes. A strange sort of light seemed to be coming from the eyes, and I couldn't look away.

I gulped and tried to move but I couldn't—it was as though I had been turned to stone.

They stared back at me without blinking.

For a moment I was sure I had seen right through them as a breeze rippled across. Then three hands stretched out towards me. The fingers were long, and the arms were unnaturally longer, like they could shoot out and touch objects much, much further away.

'Bnoy,' they said as one, in the same nasal accent.

They opened their palms and just stood there, waiting for me to drop something into them. Only then did I notice that all three were floating a few millimetres above the ground. When I looked even more closely,

I was sure that there was something odd about the shape of their feet.

'Bnoy,' they said again, this time in a wheedling kind of tone, almost like my friend Pulu, when he wants my cricket ball.

What *did* these strange men want from me?

5

As if pulled by an invisible string, my hand that was holding the box of Gems now stretched out towards the men. Oh, so that is what they wanted! All three of them looked at the packet hungrily but then seemed to be politely waiting for me to hand it to them. I placed it in the wispy fingers of the one who was closest to me. Briefly, my fingers touched his hand and a chill ran up my hand. He was so cold! It was like touching a block of ice. But different. Because ice is solid, and this was … well … not solid. It was like touching icy smoke.

By now the first man had shaken the packet of Gems, popped one into his mouth, and passed it to his friends. They both took out a candy each and started crunching. It was very dark, so I could not see clearly, but I was sure I could make out the sweets travelling down their throats.

The three of them kept looking at me with their large eyes, crunching down the Gems, and I realized the box was back in my hand.

Whooooshhhh!

Just then, the train standing by the platform let out a huge rush of steam. Startled, I turned to see what was happening there. The station lights were still out, and more shadowy figures were streaming out of the train.

I squinted my eyes and tried to see them more clearly. What I saw made my hair stand up on end all over again!

Each one of the people getting off the train was floating! Not one of their feet was properly on the ground. They all seemed to be only skimming the top of the station platform. As I watched, my mouth opened wider and wider. I was feeling a bit scared now.

'Hnello frienndssss …'

The old man who had been sitting on the bench next to me suddenly spoke, and I almost fell off the bench. But who was he talking to? Which friends?

The three men who had taken the Gems from me were smiling and nodding at him. They too looked much sharper now, their edges not so blurry, and their feet were planted on the ground as well. They had lost their sad and frightened stare and were happily smiling and waving at the old man.

'Who are you all?' I finally blurted out. None of this was making sense.

'Dnear bnoy.' They all turned to me and gave me fond smiles, like I was their long-lost friend.

'Ahem,' the old man cleared his throat, 'we are bhoots.'

What! Whoever heard of ghosts lurking around at the busy Sealdah station, sleeping wrapped up in a scratchy blanket and then taking Gems from strange boys? And who has ever heard of a ghost actually say so clearly that they are a bhoot? Aren't ghosts supposed to deceive you? Make you think they are human and then lure you to your death by breaking your neck?

'You? A bhoot?' The words just flew out of my mouth. I know it must have been rude, but really, this was all getting a bit too much.

But the men did not mind. All four of them nodded together, apparently agreeing.

I was standing at the station with ghosts! Gems-eating ghosts!

'I didn't know ghosts liked Gems,' I said suspiciously.

'Mishti ...' they chorused.

They liked sweets! Who knew!

Having solved one mystery but still feeling like I was in a very realistic dream, I looked all around me. The station was dark with the eerie moonlight washing over it. Everything looked dull, as if leached of all colour. The train was making all kinds of snorty sounds and more and more people were getting off it still. How had so many of them packed themselves into the train?

It was clear to me now that all these people were ghosts and spirits as well. My one question was, did they all want Gems so they could look more solid?

And what was the mystery of the red-coloured Gem that had jumped out at me from the box?

I just stood there, thinking deeply, holding the Gems and the comic in my hand, when I felt a tap on my shoulder.

I spun around. Then I heaved a sigh of relief at what I saw. Mama! At last, something normal. He would be able to clear up the mystery for me.

'Mama!' I was about to throw my arms around his waist in relief. But I stopped. Hadn't Mama been wearing his usual trousers and shirt and chappal when we left the house? He always wore the same brown trousers and off-white shirt. Ma was forever complaining that he never once wore the clothes she got him for the Pujas or for his birthday. But now, Mama was looking completely different. He seemed to have grown even taller, and he was wearing dhoti and kurta. Just like the ghosts!

He had on a rather fancy-looking white dhoti with a broad, decorative border. On his feet were sturdy black shoes that looked like the kind one could walk miles in. His clothes looked much cleaner than the ghosts'. But why had he changed?

A thought struck me like a wet bag of potatoes, and my heart sank.

Was Mama a ghost as well?

I looked at him closely. No, he looked the same as ever. He didn't have the transparent look of the others. He was definitely solid. And that glint in his eyes had to be real. It held lots of answers to these mysteries, and was not at all ghostly.

'Nope, not a ghost, Poltu,' he smiled, patting me on my head. 'But a ghost traffic warden.'

I gulped.

What did *that* mean?

6

There was no time to ask Mama what he meant because right then the train let out yet another long and loud hoot, which nearly burst my eardrums. The sound also disturbed the lines of wraith-like figures streaming out of the train, and they started buzzing around like a hive of bees upset by a flying cricket ball. There was a low humming sound, and the floating people seemed to get confused and started knocking into each other. Of course, there was no sound when they bumped into one another. They just gently bounced off their neighbours.

'Poltu, hang on to this.' Mama's voice was urgent as he handed me a small cloth bag. It was brightly embroidered and was closed at the mouth with a string.

I took the bag from Mama's hand and watched him rush towards the engine. 'Stay right there, Poltu!' he called over his shoulder as I started to follow him. 'I will be back in a few minutes! Don't move.'

So that was it. There was nothing for me to do now but stand in the middle of the platform, holding a funny cloth bag, my almost-empty packet of Gems and my comics under my arms, and stare at all that was happening around me. The travellers were still silently floating helter-skelter. It was difficult to make out their faces and their expressions, because everything was so ... wavy, but I could not help feeling sorry for them. They needed some help, that was for sure. Should I give them Gems?

'Bnoy ...'

I jumped. I had completely forgotten my four friends from earlier—the quiet Gems-eating bhoots. They had been standing silently all this while behind me, watching Mama and me talk to each other. They had almost melted away into the background. It was only when I realized that they were still there that I could see them clearly again.

I felt bad for ignoring them like this. It seemed rude. So I smiled. They looked delighted. Their eyes lit up. I mean, *really* lit up, like little Puja pandal toony-bulbs.

'I am Poltu,' I told them. 'I am eight and a half years old. What are your names?'

'He wants to know our names!' the first bhoot—the one who had been sleeping when I first saw him—said to the other three, delight pouring out of every word.

'I am Khepa,' he said with a little bow.

'Lalmoni,' bobbed one of the three I met later.

'Bhola,' said another, shyly.

'Ahem, Surjakumar Saif Simon W.,' announced the last one, his chest puffed up. 'But you can call me Surja.'

I nodded happily. Somehow I no longer felt scared or worried about all that was happening around me. Khepa, Lalmoni, Bhola, Surja. They were all bobbing up and down on their toes and swaying, smiles playing on their faces.

'So, what is happening?' I asked them. The train passengers were still doing their buzzing bee act, and there was still no sign of my 'traffic warden' Mama. 'Who are all these people? And where has this train come from?'

Khepa, who seemed to be the least shy of the four, looked sadly at the crowd all around us. 'Homeless bhoot,' he said with a sigh.

What did that mean? Do ghosts need a home? Can't they just live on the top of trees, or any old broken-down house? What do they need a home for anyway? They don't feel the heat or cold, or rain. They could just float around from here to there, couldn't they?

My four friends must have understood my confusion, and they all started explaining together. Now that they had had their fill of the Gems, they could speak much more clearly and loudly.

'We love big old trees. Palm trees, coconut trees, pipal trees. But trees cut. More and more. So homes are going.'

'We love deserted old houses. Tall houses, old houses, houses with roofs caving in, houses with no windows. But old houses going. Breaking old houses to make new houses filled with people, taking away homes of us bhoots.'

'We love empty fields. Only the paddy growing, the water and mud as our bed, one or two farmers. The call of nightbirds. The squelch of mud on hot summer nights. But farmers are leaving. Fields are going. Roads are coming with lots cars and trucks. Where will we sleep?'

'We love floating in small rivers and ponds. Small fish, big fish, us bhoots, all friends. But rivers are so dirty. Ponds drained of fish. No friends. We are so sad, that we have to leave.'

I stared at them in wonder. Well, who would have thought? Here in the city, we see so many homeless people, living on the streets, sleeping on the footpath. Near our house, under the old neem tree lives old Buri Dida. She's been there since forever. She stays quietly there, watches us play, and when it rains, folds her few clothes and blankets and sleeps on Nepa's balcony. His parents don't mind. As soon as the rain stops, she goes back to her spot. Someone or the other in the paara gives her food, and I have noticed she makes sure to feed the mynahs and crows and sparrows from her share. Sometimes I have heard her singing to herself. They are old folk devotional songs, Ma told me. When I get down from the school bus at the end of the lane, by Buri Dida's tree, I always know I am safely back home.

But I never ever imagined that there were so many *ghosts* wandering around looking for homes! Really, I had not thought of trees and old houses and fields and ponds as homes for anything other than birds and bats and fish and foxes. Yet, with every tree cut and every new road being laid and every river becoming dirty, it was the home of a poor ghost that was being destroyed!

All these thoughts whirled around in my head. The four of them didn't look angry or upset. In fact, they looked a bit sad. And worried. Perhaps they were worried I would cry or something. I quickly shut my mouth and gulped. I wasn't sure what to say.

How did Mama fit into all this?

One of my new ghost friends, Surja, had the kindest smile. He seemed to understand my question. 'Shankar Babu helped us,' he offered. Mama helped them? How?

The four again started on a story told in four parts.

'I was a young bhoot in the village,' started Khepa. 'Living in an o-o-o-ld house. One day, a big crane came and broke house. I ran from room to room. First downstairs. Then upstairs. Then terrace. But whole house broken by crane. What could I do? Where to stay? I took the train and came to Kolkata. Mama Babu met me at the station. Said, "Now you are assistant to me. Live on bench. Meet new bhoots. We will help them together." Now I am o-o-o-ld bhoot. Many friends.'

What a story!

'Aaaiee was branch manager,' Lalmoni started. I looked at him in awe. A branch manager is an important person, right? Manages offices and such. Lalmoni understood and gave what seemed like a wink. 'Aaaiee managed the branches of the aam gaach.'

I gave a snort of laughter. He was funny! He only managed the branches of a mango tree he lived on. Lalmoni's eyes dimmed. 'Whaan daay, tree was cut. All trees cut. Ground dug. It was mine.'

I stared at him. What was his?

'Machines, mine,' he offered.

His forest was cut to make place for a mine! Who knew ghosts did wordplay. I looked at Lalmoni with fresh respect and said, 'And let me guess. You took a train. Mama met you here, and now you help new bhoots.'

Lalmoni gave a formal bow.

Bhola was hopping from one foot to another. Sort of like when I knew an answer to a question in class and wanted to tell the teacher.

'Dam. River.'

By now I was catching on to these clever ghosts. He was not using a swear word. A dam was built on his river. 'Fish. Gone.' Bhola looked so sad. Were the fish his friends? Or did he just … like to eat them? I wanted to reach across and pat him and offer him some rui kalia.

'What about you, Surja-da?' The last of the four was already my favourite. I just knew we were going to be friends. After eating the Gems and becoming my friend, I now saw that he had a big and brilliant smile. In fact, he reminded me of one of those actors from the black and white Bengali movies Ma likes to watch on Sunday afternoons.

'Very long story. Surja very very old. Lost in the big city. Went here, went there. Saw so many things.' Surja-da's eyes looked far into a sad past. Then he winked at me. 'All Kolkata bhoots my friend. Come to Kolkata with me.'

Ummm ... sure. Why not see my own city with a knowledgeable ghost?

Just as I was about to ask him more, a voice called out from far away. Almost with a jolt, I was back in Sealdah station, with a million ghosts buzzing around me. Who was calling me?

'Poltu! Poltu! Where are you?' It was Mama's voice. Startled, I looked around. There he was, running towards me, waving.

'Yes, Mama, I am here,' I waved back.

Mama rushed up. 'Poltu, there is a lot of work tonight. I need your help.'

I stood up straighter. These were the words for which I had been preparing since I read my first Feluda. Or my first Percy Jackson. A quest! I was a hero. Of course I was ready to help. There was work to be done, and

Mama needed me. I guessed it had something to do with homeless ghosts. I—Shriman Palash Ranjan Sen aka Poltu, the quickest draw for Gems, the fastest reader of new comics, the best catcher in our paara cricket team— was ready for my first adventure.

7

'Give me the bag,' Mama panted. I had almost forgotten the little cloth bag he had handed me. I gave it to him and he peered into it. Then he heaved a sigh of relief.

'Okay, I thought I had forgotten the torch, but it's here.'

Huh? Why would he need a torch? And didn't ghosts prefer the dark anyway? But before I could say anything, Mama had drawn out a small black torch from the bag. Then he plunged into the thickest part of the bobbing crowd of ghosts.

'Follow me!' he called out. I rushed off after him, taking a second to look for my four new friends. They were floating right behind me.

'What do we need to do?' I asked as I caught up with Mama, who was making his way to the head of the train.

'Every once in a while, something sets off an influx of new arrivals,' he said, still walking very fast. 'I think this time it was that huge storm in the Sundarbans area, two weeks back.' He waved to someone further up ahead. 'But,' he slowed a bit so I could catch up, 'I was not expecting such a huge crowd tonight. A full train!'

'Does that mean they all lost their homes at the same time?' I asked.

Mama nodded. 'It was not just the storm perhaps, but some other reasons. Sometimes they wait around in lonely spots not knowing what to do. Then they see others gathering and hear about the train. But now, we need to find the Leader and show them the light.'

It all sounded rather grand to me. Show them the light?

Behind me, Khepa set off a low moan.

'What is it?' I turned to ask him.

'Shnordar is shnordarni,' he rumbled. He looked like he wanted to go back to his bench and pull the scratchy blanket over his head.

I frowned. There was no time to decipher this cryptic talk.

Surja-da floated up. From what he said, I gathered that every train load is met by the traffic warden, and one person chosen from a ghostly pool of leaders. It was usually done by lottery. My four new friends were the assistants. They lived in the station waiting for the trains and to help the Leader of the day.

They all looked a bit nervous as we approached the train. I saw Mama a little way ahead, talking to a person. Strangely, I could not see the face of the person he was talking to. In fact, I could not even see if there was a head.

I caught up with him and stood, looking from behind his waist. As I peeped, I clutched Mama's trousers hard. This could not be! The person he was talking to? Had. No. Head.

Mama placed a comforting hand on my shoulder. My own head was all topsy-turvy and I wondered if it might fall off any time now thanks to all that I was seeing tonight. But Mama looked completely relaxed talking to the headless person, so I figured this must be someone harmless, if a bit gross.

He gently pushed me forward. 'This is my nephew, Poltu. He got the red Gems today.'

The headless body turned towards me and I assumed it was 'looking' at me.

'Good,' said a firm voice. The voice was of a woman, and it was mellifluous (I read this word recently and had been wanting to use it ever since. Who knew it would be to describe someone like this?). The voice was also clear and commanding—that of a leader.

Mama was looking into the crowd all around. He had forgotten to tell me who this person was after introducing me to them. I followed his gaze. The buzzing and bobbing in the crowd had become a bit more agitated, as if they were getting impatient.

I gulped. I was not sure I wanted to be caught in the middle of a mob of angry ghosts.

'We need to get them into smaller groups,' the headless person said to Mama. 'And fast.'

Mama quickly nodded and beckoned to the four behind me. They had been hanging out there, as quiet as could be.

They darted nervous glances at the Leader. I figured I would be scared too, if my boss was headless. I could usually make out how annoyed Ma was with me from my first glimpse of her nose. Ma's nose is like a beacon, the ones we see on the tops of police cars. When it is red and flashing, it means the same as when a police car with flashing lights is behind you: get out of the way.

That is to say, if one can't see a face, how does one know what the person is going to do next?

My answer came in a moment.

On top of the headless body, a huge loudspeaker appeared.

Then there was a violent screeching. I nearly expected our paara Dada, Jhontuda, to start saying 'Mike testing 1, 2, 3 ...'

But there was no such need. The loudspeaker was working fine.

'Friends!' came the voice. That one word was enough to quieten everyone and get their attention.

'I know this has been a difficult time for you,' she said. 'I, too, have been in your place a few hundred years ago. So have my assistants. Do not worry. Everyone will get a new home. We will find them for you. Now, all of you, look at this torch held by our Chief Warden. This light will show you the way.'

And with this, the loudspeaker vanished. In its place floated a signboard. The Leader went and stood next to Mama, who in turn held up the old black torch. It flashed. The number 1 floated on the signboard in big neon lights. Khepa was floating around. He immediately rounded up and made a group of new bhoots. They were group 1.

Like this groups 2, 3, 4 were formed. Almost everyone was now in one of them, except a little lot of five or six figures. 'Today there are too many, so we could not fit everyone in.' The loudspeaker was back. 'But fortunately, today we also got a new junior warden. Our new Red Gems ... Shriman Poltu Sen!'

I? *I* was the new junior warden? A sea of ghosts looked at me. I tried to see into their eyes. Some had glittering red eyes, others only had empty eye sockets. I felt their waves of sadness and worry. I didn't know what I was supposed to do ... but I knew I wanted to help them.

8

'Go on,' Mama mouthed to me from where he was standing, holding the torch. He looked encouraging, like when he told me I could chase geckos out of the house rather than scream and hide behind someone. I took courage. I gulped. I puffed out my chest and thought about what Phantom would do. Sure, he was the 'Ghost who Walks' but did he ever have to walk *with* ghosts?

Pushing such useless thoughts aside, I walked up to the last group. They wavered in place so much, like the flickering flame of a candle, it was difficult to count them. But I looked closely and realized there were six of them in all.

I found that the Leader was next to me. I flinched and moved away an inch. It is rather hard being normal around a headless boss.

'Poltu, here is what you have to do,' she said. Surprisingly, her voice was warm. If she had a head, I think she would have nodded at me. I paid attention to the words. I had been chosen ... by the Gems ... and I needed to do my bit.

'You need to find a home for them before the sun comes up,' she said. 'We ghosts can think and move as long as it is dark. But as soon as the morning comes, we have to find the darkest corners wherever we are and sleep. If we don't have a place to go to at daybreak, we will just vanish like a puff of smoke. After that, it is anyone's guess where we may end up. We have no control over it. Once, I stayed out too late and ended up in the maths class of a school. I had to sit through trigonometry for two hours.' The shoulders shuddered delicately at the memory. 'But Poltu, I was not new to the city then, so I could make my way back to my friends and to the station. These ghosts are all new. They have already lost their homes. Now if we lose them here, in this huge city, we may never get to see them again. A lost and angry ghost can do a lot of harm, Poltu. We don't want that. We need to live among the humans without them knowing we are there. We want the ghosts safe, not worried. All they need are quiet corners—an empty room, a safe branch, an abandoned well—do you understand?'

These words played out almost directly into my mind. Suddenly, I knew a lot more about ghost life than ever before. But where was I going to find abandoned wells and safe branches for them? I mean I *was* 8.5 years old and Ma had only just started allowing me to walk home from the bus stop on my own.

By now Mama had appeared by my side as well. 'Don't worry, Poltu Singh!' He was smiling, using his special name for me. Somehow when Mama said I could do something, I felt it was true. Not like when other adults said these things.

'I have to take that big group over there.' He pointed to what appeared to be a milling crowd of about twenty ghosts standing around together. 'And our Leader has to remain at the station just in case any more strays wander in later. So tonight, your assistant will be Surjakumar.'

Surja-da appeared by my side, his warm smile still lingering on his face. He floated like a hopping smoke wisp by me and I felt a little more confident.

'But where do I start, Mama?' I asked.

'Every group is assigned an area. But since Kolkata is so big, and there are always nooks and crannies to go to, we find places for all,' Mama replied. 'Today the crowd is rather large ... but not to worry! Here are more Gems. Give everyone a red Gems before you start. Then they will all be able to speak better and you will be able to see them clearly. Here is your list, here is your own torch, keep this water bottle with you, and I will see you back here at six in the morning! By then, I will decide what to tell your mother about our train ...'

Handing me a small bag of my own, Mama hurried away to his buzzing group of ghosts. In a moment he was swallowed up in that crowd as they closed in around him. I was on my own for the night.

Wait, he had said 'list'. What list? I put my hand into the bag, but I was interrupted by a hiss. It was one of the ghosts—a very agitated man. Quickly I forgot about the list, and just stared at him.

'Ssssoooooo wayerrrrrr weeeeelllllll weeeeee gooooooo ...' His words were like little bits of wind being stirred up around us.

I cleared my throat. I was the leader of this group. I needed to act like one. They were depending on me to find them wells and branches. Surja-da floated closer to me to give me courage. I could do this.

I said more confidently than I felt, 'Please everyone, don't worry. We have a plan. I have a list. As soon as I read it, we can get going.'

The wavering circle of bodies thrummed in excitement at my words. I felt sorry for them. Just a few days earlier, they were happily haunting their old homes. And now they had to find new homes to haunt in a vast city.

Surja-da went among them and his presence seemed to calm them some more. My fingers closed in around a piece of paper in the bag and I drew it out. It was too dark to read here, so I switched on my torch. Here is what was written on the paper:

Cemetery
Old tree in park
Howrah Bridge
Old well
To return, shout out 12 times table.
For any other assistance, look within.

I stared at this gibberish. *This* was going to help me take these homeless ghosts to safety? Really, Mama?

I looked around so I could ask him to explain more. Which cemetery, which tree? Why the 12 times table? And 'look within'? Was this the time for a talk on self-confidence? I would think not!

But Mama was nowhere to be seen. The other groups too were slowly making their way away from the station, led by Khepa, Lalmoni, Bhola and some other assistant ghosts who had drifted up. I was on my own. I had to figure this out for myself.

A massive city. One ghost to help me. Six sad ghosts who needed a home. Before sunrise.

Brilliant.

I decided to start by handing out the Gems to my group. Helpfully, all the red ones jumped out at once. As the ghosts swallowed them, they became less wavy. Now instead of seeing just smoke, I could make out their features and clothes. It was a good time to leave the station and start finding my way to the places on the list.

'Follow me,' I said loudly to my group. And together we started walking and floating to the exit gates. The station was still strangely empty, like a magic curtain had fallen over it, and we were walking on a layer hidden from all ordinary passengers and porters. I guess the Leader worked this magic every time a train came in with the refugees. Imagine the chaos if all the new confused ghosts had to deal with the lights and hullabaloo of a train station right away!

The exit gates opened and we streamed out. I was wondering which way to turn, when Surja-da mumbled, 'Watch out!'

Just in time! A yellow Ambassador taxi had come racing out of nowhere and screeched to a halt where my toes had been a second ago. I could not see the driver, but the car stood there, its engine groaning and hissing. Then, with a bang, all four doors flung open.

This was our ride, I guessed. The problem was, there was no driver.

9

'Gariahat BBD Bagh. Gariahat BBD Bagh. Uthun uthun. Ektu chepey.' An electronic kind of voice sang out of the taxi. I stared at it. This was how the conductors in the minibuses that hurtled around the city yelled as people got in. Why was the taxi acting like a bus?

The taxi let out a very loud honk which caused my ghost wards to fly up in the air like a flock of frantic pigeons. 'Come back!' I called out, and they slowly settled back around me. Some were now peeping inside the cab, looking nervous. I was nervous too.

'Everyone, let's get in, let's find our first home!' I called, ignoring the wobble in my own voice.

Gingerly, one by one, and then in a rush, the ghosts swept into the taxi. Since they took up as much space as a wisp of smoke would—meaning, hardly any space—we all fit in quite comfortably.

I ran around to the front passenger side and hopped in. Truth be told, I was pretty excited! Ma never allowed me to ride up front, and here I was, all on my own, the leader of my own group, sitting importantly next to the driver!

Wait, driver? Where was the driver? The driver's seat was still empty. Surely, surely, it would be too much to expect *me* to drive as well? In reply to my silent questions, the electronic voice sang out again, 'Cholun cholun, aste aste, egiye jaan.'

Why was it hurrying us and telling us to slow down and keep moving ahead all at the same time? I cleared my throat. 'Taxiji,' I said as normally as I could to a steering wheel, 'hum jayenge cemetery.' I have no idea why I started speaking in Hindi, but that's how Ma spoke. I hoped a driver would appear from somewhere and start driving. Instead, I now noticed a bank of colourful lights on the dashboard in front, merrily winking red, yellow, and blue. They winked a little faster, and with lots of squeaks and grinding sounds, the taxi started moving!

I watched, astonished. It was good we were out and about in the middle of the night. Kolkata's taxis rarely follow traffic rules, and this one was driving itself. God only knows where it would take us. Well, we would know soon enough.

I looked out of the open window at the city at night. It was an ordinary evening when we left home and came to the station. The roads had been full of honking cars and buses. People were everywhere. This was Kolkata, after all—perhaps the busiest, most crowded place on earth. Yet now, all I could see was a thin layer of mist or smoke wrapping the city. At first I thought the roads were empty. The street lights were on, but the lights were hazy. I squinted and looked carefully out of the taxi window. The streets were actually not as empty as I had thought at first! There were shadowy figures flitting around but they vanished before I could make out who they were. It was as if I was seeing them through a screen. When we passed below a row of big trees, I was quite sure I saw a few eyes blinking down from them. Here and there on the road, people were sleeping under blankets. Perhaps they were tired ghosts. Was this the Leader's magic at work and now I could see all the other ghosts who lived in the city?

For the sake of any human pedestrians, I hoped some magic was at work, because now our taxi was bouncing along merrily down the streets of central Kolkata. I looked back at my carload of ghosts. I had not had the time to get to know them yet. It might be a good idea to do so now.

They were all sitting bunched together in the back seat. I smiled encouragingly at them. I tried to imagine what it must be like to suddenly be homeless—nowhere to hang upside down peacefully, no quiet corner to lurk in and jump out screaming 'boo!'. I felt sad.

'Kheee khee khee ... heheehe heheehe ...' I had never seen such a merry bunch of ghosts ever. Well, considering I had just met ghosts, my experience with them was not too vast, but still. So far all the ghosts I had met had been worried, sad, friendly, sometimes scary, but here was a happy bunch, nudging and pushing each other off the seat, falling on the floor of the taxi and slithering wispily about like smoke from a dhunuchi. I wondered what they had found funny, but was glad someone was enjoying this strange adventure we were on. I would have to keep this lot together.

The ghost who had spoken to me earlier was looking at me unblinkingly. I realized I didn't know whether ghosts could blink or not. I nodded at him. Next to him sat a boy ghost, no more than twelve, and I wondered why he was a ghost so young. He seemed to be practising cricketing strokes with an invisible bat. Maybe I should

find him a place on the Maidan, a nice dense tree from where he can haunt the local cricket teams. He could float over to Eden Gardens too.

Beside them sat an oldish lady. She looked like she could be chubby, though she was smoke-like like all the others. There was a kind look about her, a bit like my Thamma. My grandma came and stayed with us often and made me all the superb food Ma was always too busy to make—deemer devil, moghlai porota, fish chop, malpoa … you get the idea. I had a feeling my Thamma may not take too kindly to being compared to a ghost, but this granny ghost really did look like she would bundle me off to bed and tell me a story if she could.

I noticed Surja-da was patting a ghost encouragingly and looking at me. She was even more transparent than the others, like a piece of paper that would fly off any time. She winked in and out on the seat. Looking at her I could make out nothing—was she happy or sad? Would she like branches or wells? She was—and here I was astonished that I could use another new word I had learnt—an enigma. It means mysterious, something you can't understand, like Singh sir teaching fractions.

As my mind started drifting towards my maths holiday homework, a horrible screeching sound broke out in the car. The various loose parts of the taxi had been creating enough of a racket as it trundled down the empty and potholed roads, but now—'EEEEEEE!'

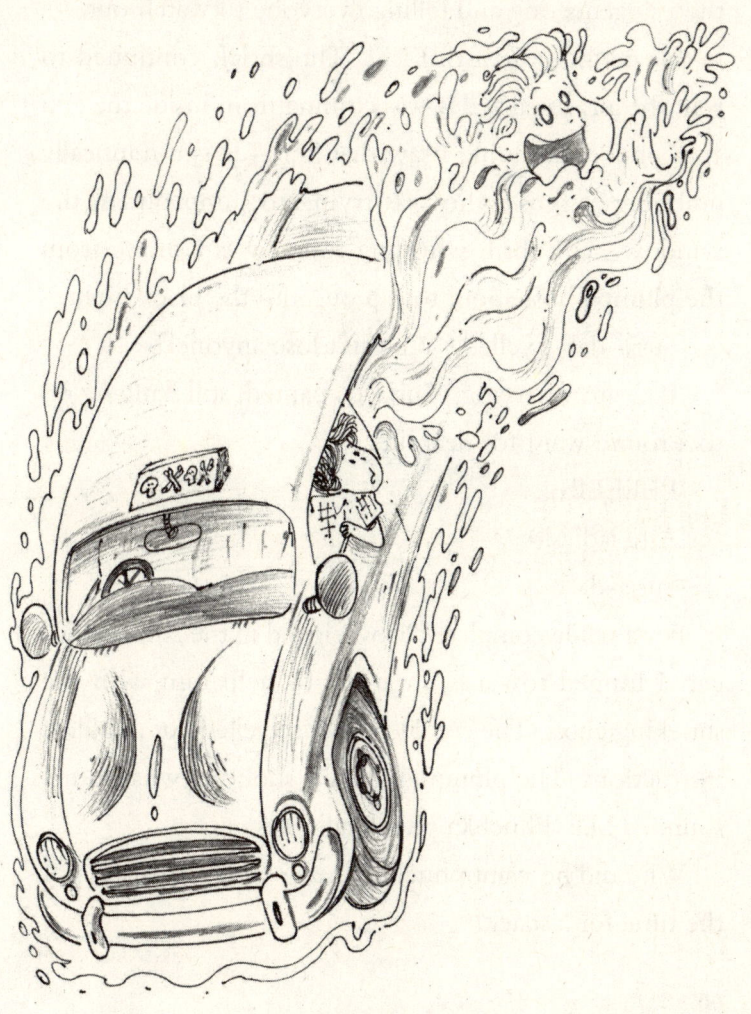

The bank of lights on the dashboard winked madly. The conductor-voice sounded agitated, 'Khuchro hobey na, cholbey na, ektu dekhey ...' It was even more garbled than ever, declaring by turns that there was no change, then sloganeering and telling everyone to watch out.

Meanwhile, 'EEEEEEE!' The shriek continued to rent the air. I realized it was coming from inside the taxi and, on a closer look, I saw that Surja-da was frantically grabbing a ghost who was trying to jump out of the window. The shrill whistling sound was coming from the plump ghost about to slip out into the black night.

'Surja-da!' I yelled. 'We can't lose anyone!'

'I ... am ... trying,' Surja-da panted, still hanging on to a round waist for dear life.

'EEEEEEE!'

'Aste ladies!'

'Surja-da!'

For a while complete chaos reigned in the Ambassador car. I lunged towards Surja-da, to help him with the shrieking ghost. The conductor-voice yelled out muddled instructions. The plump ghost was shouting what to me sounded like 'Phuchka phuchka!'

Why did he want phuchkas now? Surely this was not the time for a snack!

Slowly the shrieks died down. The escaping ghost got back fully in the car. I noticed his face for the first time. His cheeks were now trembling in some sorrow.

Oh dear, was he missing home so much that he had wanted to fly out of the car and go back all the way? Had he been separated from a ghost friend whom he missed?

A little sob escaped him.

'Alu kabli.'

Huh? Did he want to have chaat now? Why had he been yelling for phuchkas earlier?

'What's up? Hello, can I help you?' I asked, weakly.

'Ghugni,' he sobbed out. 'Jhal muri. Ra … dha … balla … bi ….' And now he broke into wild tears.

I scratched my head. The ghost was reciting the best of Kolkata's street foods. Was he perhaps … hungry?

Surja-da must have been watching me and seen the light dawn in my eyes.

'He saw a phuchka stand,' he said simply.

That explained it. I have cousins and even an aunt who did not behave too differently when they came to Kolkata. I had to stop them from stuffing their faces at every street corner with unhealthy chaat and spicy foods every time we stepped out.

'Thanks, Surja-da.' Then I looked at the ghost whose eyes were brimming with unshed tears. 'We will stop soon,' I said. What was the point in being carted off to a city like Kolkata, and not even get to eat a shingara? While Surja-da patted the ghost's arm and pointed out some jamun trees that bore healthy fruits, I realized our conductor had started to recite a list of new names.

'Belgharia Esplanade Moulali Chowringhee,' he was saying. But the merry edge was no longer there in his voice. He sounded somewhat scared. I wondered why.

And then I looked ahead and knew.

This place could scare anyone. It was the South Park Street Cemetery I had crossed on the way to the train station a few hours earlier. At that time, the road outside had been jampacked. Now, nothing moved but bits of stray paper in the wind. Tall dark trees rustled their leaves menacingly. The wall around the cemetery loomed up. Huge branches bent low over the walls. Through the gate, I saw a row of tombs lined up inside.

We were here—perhaps the first home for my group.

I said a short prayer and opened the car door. The rest of the ghosts had streamed out of the open windows. We gathered together at the gate.

'Lake Town,' the taxi squeaked in a soft tone and rattled off to park itself.

10

One of my favourite books is a Feluda detective novel called *Gorosthaney Shabdhan*. In it, Feluda, Topshe and Lalmohan Babu solve a mystery that takes place around this very cemetery. So, I knew the place somewhat, if only from the book. Mama had also told me that it was the cemetery for the first Europeans who came to India. There are graves here of people who died in the 1700s. The cemetery filled up by the 1880s, and has now become a bit of a tourist spot. I had seen some photos on Google with Mama—some of the tombstones were as big as houses! Mama had said that the more important the person, the bigger they wanted the tombs to be. It is a sad kind of place, but also quiet and filled with large trees that sigh and rustle.

The tombs are scattered all over the area. If you read the names on them, you can see that some belong to entire families. Some are plain, others are ornamented. There is one that looks, strangely, like an old-style temple. During monsoons, Mama told me, the ground is slippery with green moss.

Ever since I read the Feluda mystery story, I'd been wanting to come here and solve an age-old puzzle like my favourite detective.

Little did I know that I would be standing at the gates one day, on a very different kind of mission. My group flickered and drew closer to each other. Something was making them nervous. I took a step forward. Beyond the big iron gate, there was a small office where I guessed a guard sat during the day. Now, there was no one.

And yet, the gate creaked open.

I cleared my throat, squared my shoulders, checked that my bag with the torch was there, and stepped through the gate. Surja-da was making sure everyone else clung close to me. They were now one big misty clump, moving together like a large ball. Good.

How would I know if a place was the correct home for my ghosts? What went into getting them into a new home? Did I just leave a ghost there and say goodbye?

Was there a paper to sign off? I felt a bit miffed at the Leader and Mama for leaving zero clues on this.

The cemetery was nearly in complete darkness. Some bits of light were coming in through the trees from the street. I thought I heard our taxi softly moan more street names. Maybe that was its way of saying good luck.

This was it. I had to rely on my own wits—like Tintin. I took one more step. Nothing happened. The place remained as quiet as a ... well, graveyard. I took a few more steps. With each one I felt a small burst of confidence. This was it! I just had to make sure my ghosts were settled, and then I would make my way back to the station, well before the sun rose. Maybe we would even take the next train out to Jalpaiguri. So easy!

Even as all these thoughts crowded my mind, the dark night was sliced in two—not by light, but by a shining white wall. We stopped short. An angry moan was travelling up and down the wall, as it trembled and heaved. It was as if all the hurt and sadness in the world had been concentrated and then thrown on us like a cold bucket of water. I felt all my confidence drain away—how would I fight a wall of sadness?

A sob came from the ball of ghosts behind me. Truth be told, I wanted to turn around and run back myself—

back to Ma, back to our small and cosy home where the smell of her talcum powder hung in the air, where there was always a comforting plate of dal bhaat and alu bhaja. Oh, what I would do to get a nice hot plate of alu bhaja now. No … why was I thinking of food? And why was my head spinning, as more and more visions of food crowded my mind—luchi, pulao, kosha mangsho, chowmein, roll, chop, cutlet … What was happening to me? Was I going mad? Had the hungry plump bhoot taken over my mind?

Then I saw that the wall had stopped rippling. Instead, it was now separating into ghostly forms. There was a woman in a long old-fashioned dress, like in the movies that Ma watched. There were men dressed in tight pants and coats and hats which had plumes of feathers fluttering. There were so many of them! Twenty? Fifty? It was impossible to count as they kept merging into each other, then separating out. They would bow to one another, raise their hats, and mill around some more.

After greeting each other they all turned towards us and froze in their place, shimmering slowly.

Surja-da leaned into my ear and whispered, 'Think of roast mutton.'

Seriously? What was it about these ghosts and food? First phuchka, then my own mind going berserk thinking

about the food at home. And now roast mutton. What was roast mutton? I had read about it in books. Like I had read about tongue sandwiches and bullseyes and glistening hams in Enid Blyton books but I had never really seen any of them.

'Stop right there!' a voice rang out from among the cemetery ghost crowd. It sounded different, the way people in the English movies spoke. But it was also rough and papery, like it was very, very old.

One of the ghosts stepped forward. He was tall and had a pistol tucked into his belt. There was a patch of black on his forehead. Then I looked carefully and my breath nearly stopped. It was not a patch but a hole that one could see right through! I shuddered.

'Where do you think you are going?' he demanded, not in a very kind voice.

'I ... I ...' I stammered. All the words flew out of my head on seeing the dark hole in his head. I wished Surja-da had given me better advice than 'roast mutton'.

'You see,' I started to explain. 'My friends here are newly arrived ghosts ...'

'No no, nahin nahin. Nahin chalega. Jao tum jao. Yeh European cemetery. No Indian ghosts allowed here.' The man was getting angrier and angrier, puffing up with each

word. All the other foreign-looking ghosts had gathered around him and were nodding away furiously.

I stared at them in dismay. Did they not know that India had been independent now for decades? That you could not stop Indians from going anywhere in our own country? Behind me, my ghost ball also buzzed angrily. I could see a few hands among the Europeans reaching for their pistols and swords that clanged at their sides.

There were easily fifty of them. And we were a ball of ghosts and me.

How would we take them on in a battle? How *did* one fight ghosts in a battle, I wondered.

But there was no time. They had formed a wall again and were moving towards us, like they meant to drive us away forever.

And then, almost all at the same time, the following words rang out.

'Surja-da!' That was me.

'Sssssstop!' That was someone from my ghost group.

'Beef goulash!' That was Surja-da.

Like a whiplash, these words seemed to strike our opponents. They came to a sudden halt. The wall stopped in its tracks.

A ghost stepped up. 'What did you say?' Her voice was kinder, softer.

'Umm ... Surja-da?' I offered.

'Ssssstop?' my ghost friend suggested.

Surja-da stepped forward. At his side was the hungry ghost from earlier.

'Beef goulash!' they said in unison.

I sniffed the air. What was this smell? It was like warm tomato soup.

A gasp rang out. No, I was not imagining it. The cemetery ghosts looked thunderstruck. It dawned on me that they were probably hungry too. For how many centuries had they been lying here, wishing for a morsel of food from their land? No wonder they were angry. Since they'd died and gone to their graves, the land around them had changed so much. Gone were the people who came with them, their food, their clothes.

I stepped up towards Surja-da and the other ghost and took their hand. It was difficult to hold tight as it was mostly cold air, but I still hung on. Surja-da led the chant and we followed. We yelled out, 'Fish and chips!'

Immediately the air filled with the smell of fried fish. A vision of a large slab of fish encased in a golden crisp batter with fat juicy potato chips shimmered in front of my eyes.

'Oooooh …' a collective moan went up.

Now I felt another hand slip into mine. It was Thamma ghost. She smiled at me, filling me with courage, the way my grandmother did when I hid behind her if a cockroach darted in front of me.

'Moussaka!' we yelled.

What? What on earth was a moussaka and where had I learnt to say it? There was no time to think about that. For the word had created another happy stir among the cemetery lot. They didn't look ready to take us on in a fight to the finish anymore. All they wanted to do was sniff the air and stare longingly into space.

One by one, my whole ghost gang joined us and we formed a chain, holding hands. Words I had never heard before rolled out of my mouth. But Surja-da and the hungry one knew them all.

'Spaghetti and meatballs!'

'Schnitzel!'

'Shepherd's pie!'

'Steak and kidney pie!'

The air was thick with the smell of freshly cooked food—hearty and piping hot, fresh from the oven. There was the smell of newly made bread. I was sure I could even hear the sound of roast meat sizzling in the pan.

We stopped for a moment to take a deep breath, looked at each other and nodded. We knew now what would disarm our opponents fully.

I filled my lungs with air. The gang just puffed up like balloons.

And we shouted into the night air, 'Tea with a spot of milk!'

11

At the mention of tea, complete silence fell on us. But this was a nice, warm silence broken only by the sound of what sounded like spoons tinkling in a cup of tea. A circular table and some chairs had been conjured up from somewhere, and a few of the cemetery ghosts were sitting around it, chatting amiably with each other, pretending to drink tea from ghostly shimmering teacups. There was a nice big fruit cake in the middle of the table. All around us there was peace and quiet, and the fight that looked like it had been about to break out just some minutes back had evaporated.

I heaved a sigh of relief. At least I would not have to do battle with ghosts. For now.

I walked up to the ghost with the hole in his head, because he seemed to be the leader of the lot. He looked like he could be a bit mean, and I would have preferred to speak to the kindlier ghost. I noticed she was at the table now, a cup of tea next to her, smiling at me.

I cleared my throat. 'Ahem. Sir, I have some new ghosts with me. They have arrived just today. May some of them stay here with you, in this beautiful and peaceful graveyard?'

Phew! That was the longest speech I had made in English to a ghost. I was proud I had remembered all the words. I looked closely at Bullet Hole Ghost to see his reaction. His back was straight as ever, and his hand still hovered near the sword at his side. But his face was calm, so I did not panic.

'My boy!' He let out a bit of a wail. 'My boy, you have come to us after so long!'

I looked at Surja-da, who just shrugged. My ghost group had scattered a bit now, and were looking around, like they were inspecting a new home. They were staring up at the branches of the tall trees. A few were popping in and out of the little alcoves on some of the graves. One was bouncing on a slab of marble as if testing out a new bed.

'After so long someone has talked to us. You brought us a feast! The food of our homes!'

'Come, my boy, here, take this cup of tea. Join us,' the lady at the table said.

Bullet Hole Ghost was smiling peacefully, so I did as asked. The lady held out an imaginary cup of tea to me that I took from her and sipped from, just the way I did when I played with my little cousin Bulti.

'You see, every few years some new ghosts come and join us here,' she explained. 'Some years, there are too many of them, like the time the last of the British left India.'

I nodded. I knew that when India became independent, there had been riots in which people had died. Had some of those who died ended up here as ghosts?

She wiped a tear and sniffed. 'So many sad stories. But as the years went by, everything changed around us. Trees were chopped near us here too. We can hear the sound of trams and buses and cars all day and night. The night is no longer as dark as we would like it to be. There is always some light coming from somewhere, so we can't roam around as much as we used to.'

I listened to her silently. I had not thought about the problems of urban ghosts before now.

'And then, my boy,' Bullet Hole chimed in, his voice loud and booming, 'and then, those who came in here knew nothing about us! We, who have been lying here for years and years! I tell you, my boy, that hurt.'

'Um ... uh ... well ...' What was a kind way to tell a ghost that we had had a lot on our minds then? Like, you know, building a whole new nation after Independence? I still felt bad for them. It must hurt when everything changes around you, but you can't move forward or back. You are just stuck right there, in the middle of the city, where you are a part of forgotten history.

'But today!' Bullet Hole continued, and all the ghosts rose up as one, much to our alarm. The cemetery ghosts were forming a line once more. But this time it was not to form an angry wall. They were holding each other's hands and smiling and bowing. What were they going to do?

With a thud next to me, a piano appeared. I rubbed my eyes. The stern-looking ghost from our group stepped up and with a bow and flourish sat in front of the piano. He played a few notes slowly, testing out the piano. Then, the serious look went away from his face and he started smiling. He liked the piano! I wondered where he had learnt to play it. Was it when he was young and not a ghost? Cheerful music filled the air.

The ghosts smiled and bowed some more. Oh were they going to …? Yes, they were going to! They were about to … dance!

As I and my group of ghosts watched in awe, they formed a neat line and started twirling. And … was that … was that a song? Made up entirely of food names? Yes, it was, and set to a happy tune.

Who wants roast beef?
We do, we do!
Who wants a slice of pie?
We do, we do!
Who wants mincemeat?
We do, oh yes, we do!
Who wants …

(And here they jumped and flew around each other in the air in a not-scary way at all.)

Cake! Pie! Bread! Pudding!

The names of different foods came fast now as the dance got wilder. The jumping and swirling became a crazy flurry. No longer could we tell one ghost from the other. It was all one big happy musical mass.

We were also clapping along with them. Who could not help but share in this sudden moment of joy? And then, our own plump ghost stepped up and joined them.

He was quite quick on his feet as well. One by one, more of our group joined in. I just kept smiling and looking at them all.

I had always thought of ghosts as sad or scary. But perhaps they were also just like us humans—they liked to have fun, even if it was a bit of a wild rumpus.

Slowly the music wound down, and everyone flopped down on the ground. They had all become friends now—the old and new ghosts. They were joking and slapping each other on their backs, though since they were all air, their hands just went through emptiness. I guess it is the thought that counts.

Already I could see that the plump one, the formerly stern one, Thamma ghost, and the bunch of merry ghosts who had been giggling away in the taxi had made themselves quite at home. They were laughing and humming and even trying out some complicated dance moves.

I was sure now that I had succeeded in some part. I had taken them to their new home.

I saw Surja-da standing apart and watching, a slight smile on his face. He turned to me and winked. He knew too. Then he nodded towards the gate.

It was time to leave. We only had a few more hours left, and two ghosts from my group remained homeless. The cricketer boy and the silent woman still stood by me. The cricketer had been practising cricket strokes even when the dancing started. And the silent woman had stood apart the whole time, not joining in the mad singing and dancing. I guessed they wanted a different kind of home.

I walked up to the laughing ghosts. Their laughter did not sound scary at all. It was gentle and really happy, more like a soft breeze blowing through the trees making them rustle and shake. Wait, was this the sound I had heard before? Somewhere close by a ghost had been laughing? Well, well.

I shook hands (the air) with Bullet Hole Ghost. He was already chatting with Thamma ghost and telling her about the time he lost his head—literally—in a duel. Thamma was listening to him, but she also looked at me and smiled warmly. She would be all right here.

Plump ghost was at the table and showing a bunch of European ghosts how to make jhaal muri. A bag of puffed rice and various condiments like boiled potatoes, onions, peanuts, and mustard oil had appeared from nowhere. Everything was made of air but also smelt like it was real. I guess this was the closest they would get to real food. I raised a hand and waved to Plump ghost. He nodded back.

The piano ghost man was sitting at the piano surrounded by many young ghosts. It looked like he was showing them some new tunes. Was it my imagination or was that Michael Jackson's 'Thriller'?

Another bunch of happy ghosts were learning more dance steps and were engrossed in a complicated routine that seemed to involve a lot of head rolling. I left them to it.

The two remaining ghosts gathered around me and we started walking to the gate. I could see that our ghost cab had already drawn up there. It gave a few merry toots of its horn. The lights on the dashboard were winking away.

It was time to find the next home.

12

We all piled into the taxi that had lost its earlier nervousness from when it dropped us at the cemetery gate. Now it was standing at the gate again, but there was a cheery air about it. Before it went into another crazy mode of reeling off random place names, I said firmly, 'Maidan.'

The Maidan is a huge open area near Victoria Memorial where people picnic, go on buggy rides on the roads around it, and watch the many, many cricket matches played there all year round. Groups of players gather in teams and you can hear cries of 'Catch!' and 'Out!' if you walk around. Sometimes a tram may trundle by. Every winter Ma and I go there with a group of friends. We play and then we sit on the rugs we take with us and read books.

I had decided that the cricketer boy ghost would be happiest there. Even at the cemetery I had noticed that after the dancing he had wandered to a nearby patch of grass and had been pretend bowling at a cenotaph. When he swung his arms and appeared to bowl, his face was filled with happiness. I wondered what his story was. Why had he lost his home? Had he been part of a ghost cricket team before?

I really wanted to ask him, but there was no time because our taxi had decided to race another taxi that was also headed to the Maidan. The other taxi had suddenly appeared next to ours, and now the two cars zoomed and rattled and swerved around each other while I held on grimly. I was about to ask our cab to calm down, when it struck me: all this while the roads of the city had been empty. That was unusual, I knew, because Kolkata is not a city that sleeps. I had assumed that the Leader had thrown some ghost magic that had emptied it all out in order to make our task easier. So then where had this taxi come from now? And why was it chasing us?

I looked closely. The other taxi was veering dangerously close to us. It was filled with what could only be ghost people. They were all in white trousers and shirts. There seemed to be many of them piled into the car. And they were all glaring at me.

I gulped. What now? What had I done to anger a bunch of travelling ghosts?

'Taxiji?' I asked, hoping our self-driving car could provide some clue. In reply, the dashboard lights went into crazy mode, but the voice didn't say anything. Right, this was completely the time for it to shut up and drive.

I looked around at the remaining passengers in the car. They were all sitting at the back, quiet, staring out the window at the other car.

That car was now almost dashing into us from the side.

'Hey!' I yelled at it. 'Watch out!'

Hazy hands snaked out of the windows of the other taxi. Faces pushed themselves out. What on earth did they want? What was the meaning of this sudden ambush?

I thought back to what Feluda or Tintin or Phantom would do in a situation like this. Well, I did not have a Colt 32 revolver, nor a great big white horse, nor a small smart dog. Why had I set out on this adventure without a reliable companion?

Wait, I *did* have someone to help me. Surja-da! Would he have some ideas? After all, his advice on roast mutton in the cemetery had been spot on.

I called out in a shaky voice without turning around, my eyes glued to the other taxi that was now dodging in and out of our path. 'Surja-da, what should we do?'

'Park.'

Park? Like we should park the car and let them go on their own mad way? Not a bad idea. Why had I not thought of it?

'Park, park!' I yelled at our taxi.

It stopped its own weaving to stay away from the attacking cab and sputtered to a halt. Then it let out a great whoosh of smoke and switched itself off. We all let out a sigh. The other taxi sped up ahead. Hopefully we had shaken it off.

I stuck my head out of the window to check. All I could see was a distant taillight vanishing into the dark night. Phew! Who knew why they had given chase? But now they were gone and we could get going ourselves.

But wait, why was this place so dark? So far, the roads had been lit by streetlights, whose lights had been dialled down a lot, just enough for our taxi. But this spot was pitch dark.

With a wildly beating heart I looked around me, squinting and hoping to make out any shapes around us. Our car's light threw an unsteady beam that seemed to be getting swallowed by the darkness. All this while I hadn't been really scared, but now my heart thudded. Who likes to be stuck on an unknown road with a car full of ghosts in utter darkness?

'Surja-da?' I asked in a quavering voice.

'Park,' came the reply again. He sounded quite calm.

We *were* parked. Why did he keep telling us to do that?

I turned around to look at him. But Surja-da was looking elsewhere. Out of the window. He was pointing. My gaze followed his finger but I could not make out anything, it was so dark. I could barely see my ghosts. They would have been lost if not for their shimmering whiteness. Our car's lights had also dimmed quite a bit. I rubbed my eyes and looked again, willing them to adjust to the lack of light.

Slowly, some shapes came into view. They were tall. They were moving. There was a sinister rustling sound in the air. Were they ... were those trees?

By 'park', had Surja-da meant an actual park? We had to go to *a* park? For what? Ma strictly forbade me from going to our neighbourhood park where weird and unknown people sat around all day. I was certainly not going to step into one in the middle of the night!

The silence of the night was broken by a shrill scream.

We all jumped in the car. I clutched the seat, wishing I had someone solid to hang on to, not just beings of air. The taxi gave a hiccupping squeak.

Then more screams broke through the still night air. None of them made any sense.

'Caaaaaatch!'

'Out!'

'Nooooo …!'

The last scream petered out, lingering and becoming softer.

This was awful! Was someone getting hurt? What should I do?

I did not have to think much more, because with a sudden bang our taxi door flew open. My eyes, I knew, were now round as marbles.

With a whooshing sound something flew out. Was it a bat? A plane? No, it was one of our ghosts!

The cricketer ghost had rushed out of the car and, in the darkness, he was making for the trees in the distance. 'Wait!' I shouted. I wasn't going to lose a ghost on my first night on the job. What if he went off somewhere dangerous?

I threw open my car door and sprinted after him.

'Wait!' I yelled at his fast retreating back. 'Don't go alone! I am coming with you.'

But he wouldn't stop. At top speed, he was making for the bank of trees. The trees too seemed to be waving in the wind and calling to us. I even thought I heard some wild cheering going on. As though a whole crowd was egging him on.

What lay behind those trees? And would I end up a ghost myself as I chased him down?

13

I reached, panting, with a stitch in my side. As I tried to catch my breath, I saw that the park was not really a park. It was a large ground, as big as a stadium. I straightened up and looked around, and my mouth fell open. It *was* a stadium! Who knew there were two big stadiums so close to each other? I had only heard of Eden Gardens, and seen it on TV when cricket matches were shown. There was also a football stadium. But where had this one suddenly sprung up from?

As I stared, another loud cheer broke out. The crowd, I now saw, was made up of many types of smoky apparitions. Some were missing heads entirely, a bit like the Leader. There was a whole row of ghosts with unnaturally long arms. These arms were waving in the air like wobbly balloons. A few others had their

heads fixed the wrong way and sat there looking back-to-front.

There was a deafening sound everywhere. I spotted banners being waved all around, saying things like 'Rock the Deads' and 'Go Team Spirit'. There were many more but I would have to stand there gawping and squinting if I wanted to read them all—which I couldn't.

By now Surja-da was hovering next to me, and I tried to find the cricketer ghost but it was impossible. There were just too many of them, all looking sporty.

'What is going on?' I managed to yell into Surja-da's ear.

'Final game,' he said.

So this was the final game of a tournament? No wonder everyone was so excited. How astonishing that what we thought was an ordinary park could become the spot for such intense sporting action at night. I figured that by day it remained just a park like so many in the city, and by night it became a twin Eden Gardens.

I knew of one-day games and Test cricket and IPL. I wondered if ghost cricket was the same. Did they follow the same rules as us, or did they create new ones, like we did when we played on the paara street? In our games, if anyone hit the ball into a house, you were out. We also had lots of fights about whose turn it was to bat and bowl. I hoped the ghosts did not have any of these fights.

Surja-da must have realized I was thinking about this, so he said, 'Fifty-night match, each night thousand runs needed, teams of 15.5. Final game.'

Well, that made no sense at all. Who could play for fifty nights and make a thousand runs each night? And what was a half-player?

The last question was answered right away, when I saw only the legs of a player run into the ground. That was a half-player, all right.

Surja-da was still reeling off the rules.

'Make 100 runs and you are out. One over is 20 balls. 1 flying run makes 10 runs.'

He paused and looked at me and then said again, 'Final game.'

This time when he said 'final game', he looked quite grim. I wondered why he kept telling me that it was the final game. It was a bit creepy.

But there was no time to ask all these questions. Because just then a huge cloud arose from the middle of the ground. No, wait, it was not a cloud, it was a big group of ghostly bodies rising up together. There were about twenty of them, all dressed in cricketing whites, and they were whirling around in the air, shouting and slapping each other on the back.

I could not make out if the game was just starting or if they did this during the game. I guess it would be nice if the players could take a break and fly around a bit, sort of like a timeout.

By now the excitement in the crowd was getting to me too. I felt the familiar hammering in my heart that was there each time India played. The cloud of players had stopped whirring around and had landed back on the pitch. They fanned out all over the ground and one batsperson took guard. I saw a menacing-looking bowler thunder in from the other end. The ground seemed to shake as the bowler ran up. I tried to make out what she looked like but all I could see was long hair that streamed behind and from which sparks were flying up. It was a fearsome sight.

The ball flew out of her hand and, with a mighty thwack, the batter sent it flying. Immediately all the fielders started shouting at the top of their voices, 'Who WHO WHO will catch?!' The crowd joined in as well. And a rhythmic chant of 'WHO WHO WHO' filled the air.

Meanwhile, the ball went higher and higher till it seemed to disappear into the sky. I had never seen anyone hit a ball so far. I joined in with everyone, staring up into the inky darkness, waiting for the ball to come back to earth. The fielders were still milling around, their arms stretched out.

And then, like a missile, I saw that the ball was heading straight down—towards me.

'Caaaaatch! Caaaatch!' The din was unimaginable. I waited for someone to catch the ball. Airy figures ran around me. A hand reached out. But the ball was travelling too fast.

Thonk!

'OUUUUUTTTT!'

A massive shriek tore through the night.

Yes, someone was out.

It was me. The ball had landed on my head.

I saw stars. Then, complete blackout.

14

When I woke up, I tried to open my eyes but they wanted to stay glued shut. I was sleepy. I wanted to snuggle in my own comfortable bed. Why was Ma calling me? It was the holidays and it was not yet morning. But wait, why was Ma's voice like this? Why was she whispering in my ear? She never did that! My eyes stayed shut and I sank back into sleep with a pleasant whispery air in my ear. This was nice. No, wait, the whisper was saying something.

'Wake up, Poltu.'

'Wake up and take your trophy.'

'Wake up, Person of the Match.'

Trophy? Person of the match? Right, this was one of those dreams again. I was sleeping, and this was a dream, and I would keep my eyes shut so that it would not stop. I *never* got man of the match. Like ever. It was always that pesky Rinku from two houses away who could bat and bowl better than any other kid in our paara.

I would dream on, and Rinku would never get her trophy.

But now someone was shaking me. Or, not exactly shaking. It was like my body was moving on its own. With a groan, my eyes fluttered open. For a second, I looked above me. No, this was still a dream, because what I saw made no sense. Ghostly faces were peering at me.

Wait, ghosts? Wasn't I shepherding some ghosts around all night? And hadn't I lost one of them? Did I not chase him down and land in the middle of a cricket match?

It all came rushing back to me. I could not lie in my bed! I had work to do! I was on an adventure.

I sat bolt upright and looked around me.

No, I wasn't in my bed. In fact, I wasn't in *any* bed. I was lying on a hard cricket pitch. All around me were worried faces. The crowd that had earlier been yelling their lungs out was now completely hushed.

One familiar face came closer. Surja-da!

'What happened, Surja-da?' I asked.

I thought I saw a smile of relief on his face. His eyes twinkled.

'Get up and take your trophy,' he said.

There was a trophy? I had not dreamt it? But why? I had not been playing. I had only been watching when the ball had landed on my head. I stared, puzzled.

But there was no time to stare, as now I saw a very grand bhoot approaching me with a giant shiny trophy. I leapt to my feet and brushed myself down. The trophy-giving ghost was dressed in a smart pink suit, complete with a red polka-dotted bow tie at his neck. On his feet were red shoes that glistened. He had a huge grin on his face and his chubby hands clutched the trophy like he was protecting it. But what I could not stop staring at was the top of his head. It had caved in, the way a mound of mud might look if you dropped a ball in it. It didn't seem to bother him though, because his smile did not waver as he stood before me.

There was a ring of ghosts around him, all wearing dark glasses and whispering into their wrists. I guessed they were bodyguards. But why would a ghost need a bodyguard? Wasn't he already ... dead? I put aside such questions for later and smiled back nervously at him. I felt like I was up on the stage in school, getting a prize. Since my experience so far on this had been just the once, for spellings, it was a very odd feeling.

'Go on, go on. Take your trophy. You saved the day. Hahahahaha!' Many hands were propelling me forward, so I stumbled the few steps between me and the Very Important Ghost. He held out the trophy, smiling wider and wider till I was afraid the smile would spill out of his face. I held out my own shaky hands. I was still puzzled why I was getting it, but everyone was looking at me with fond eyes so I felt I had to take the trophy. Perhaps it would all become clear soon.

As soon as I took the trophy, which felt surprisingly solid, a wave of cheers shook the stadium. Screams of joy swept up and down the place, rising into a deafening din. This was worse than our school playground at break time. A booming voice announced dramatically, 'Aaaaand our chaaaampion today! Shri Poltu Sen!'

I blinked. The VIG was smiling and waving, turning round and round on his shiny shoes.

'And nowwwww!' the commentator voice started again, 'A speeeech!!'

What? Was I going to have to give a speech now? In a stadium? I looked around desperately for a way to run. This was more frightening than driving around the city with homeless ghosts. But I didn't have to worry. The call for a speech was not for me, but for the VIG. From nowhere a microphone had appeared in his hand, and he was clearing his throat in a very important manner.

This I could handle. Many important guests came to school and gave long boring speeches. Relieved, I lugged the large and heavy trophy and stood next to Surja-da.

'Ladies and gentlemen, boys and girls, my dear fellow ghosts,' the VIG started off. Everyone stopped cheering to listen.

'For years and years, this ground has seen many epic games of cricket. I remember! I remember that time, a hundred years ago, when I watched the great Happy Glower take 6 wickets in 1 ball. Yes! All you youngsters should learn! Go, watch the match again! Yes yes yes!'

And then he stopped. I listened, fascinated. I had never heard anyone speak like this in our school. And how were 6 wickets in 1 ball even possible? I had to get to know more about the rules of ghost cricket later from Surja-da.

Meanwhile, the VIG was carrying on, recounting other memorable games.

'This is the same ground, where Munil Papaskar sent a ball flying so high, *so* high, that it touched the sky. Who can ever forget that? HAVE you all seen that match? Have you? Have you have you?'

My head was spinning now at this speech and these impossible stories. But the crowd was rapt. The VIG ploughed on.

'This is the ground, which we were told we would never be able to play on again! How could that happen? This is the ground of our dearest sporting ancestors! Our galaxy of stars! And they wanted us to move! Why? Because the trees were too tall. Because the grass was too short! Because because because …'

And now the crowd chanted, a sorrowful lilt in their voices, 'Because the dead can't play.'

I felt tears rising up. There, in the cemetery, the ghosts had not been able to eat. And now in this large stadium, someone had told the ghosts they could not play. But who? And why?

'The Board of Ghost Cricket Control had told us that we create a nuisance here during the matches! They want to control all the cricket. They said: Why do you need to play sports? Go away from here. We will use the park for an exclusive club.

'But who said no? Who said no who said no who said no?

'I did!'

The crowd now went wild. But how had VIG stopped the Board?

'I said: We will do the impossible! We will play an extraordinary game, and you will not be able to move us! I said I said I said, by the Final Game, we will do the SUDDEN NOT DEATH!'

Now the crowd went completely mad. There was hooting and whistling and stamping, and I was sure I saw a few heads roll as their owners threw their own heads into the air and caught them like cricket balls. What was a sudden not death?

The VIG smiled as he turned to look at me. 'See our young friend. He doesn't know the rules yet. How many kinds of OUTs do we know?'

He took on the manner of a teacher and held up his fingers, counting off the categories one by one. The crowd repeated each one after him.

'LBW!' ... 'LBW LBW!'

'Catch!' ... 'Catch Catch!'

'Run Out!' ... 'Run Out Run Out!'

'Bowled! ... 'Bowled Bowled!'

'Aaaand?'

There was silence. Then a small voice piped up from the stands. It was the cricketer ghost from my group! I looked on proudly, though I did not understand what he was saying.

'Sudden Death!'

A refrain of 'Sudden Death' echoed around the stadium.

The VIG saw my look of wonder and launched into an explanation.

'Our young friend does not know that if the ball lands on a head it is OUT and it is called getting OUT by SUDDEN DEATH. See! See my head!'

That explained the cave-in atop his head.

'But in the rarest of rare cases, if the ball is hit just right, and the person who comes below it is just the right person then the ball knows!'

I tried to clear my ears. The ball knows? What does the ball know?

'The ball knows how to slow down and cause SUDDEN NOT DEATH! That is why that is why that is why. Shri Poltu appeared here at just the right time and stood under the correct ball. He did not BREAK HIS HEAD. And by not doing that he made it a SUDDEN NOT DEATH.'

Phew, I was glad to hear that. So, that was how I had saved a whole stadium for ghosts to play in, by getting hit on the head—but not too hard. It seemed a fairly ordinary thing to do and not deserving of such a large trophy. But I felt happy. I caught Surja-da's eyes and he nodded. I did a small wave to the crowd. Happiness was radiating everywhere, till I spotted something at the edge of the ground.

That same car! The one that had been chasing us off the road. All those menacing ghosts were now coming out of it one by one. Grimly, they floated up fast towards us. Even the VIG shuffled his feet nervously, but stood his ground.

Surja-da whispered, 'The BGCC.'

Oh so *these* were the bad guys. The ones who had wanted to control the cricket and make a club. The Board of Ghost Cricket Control.

With them gathered around us, I felt trapped. What if I had angered them by helping all the sporty ghosts?

One of them took up a mike. I really had not known that ghosts liked to give so many speeches.

'You win.'

That was all she said.

The noise that followed could have 'woken up the dead', as our English teacher sometimes complained about our class 3B. But then this *was* the dead making so much noise. I would tell Miss that—the dead are not quiet, and they don't want to lie quietly in graves. They want to eat and party and play exciting cricket. Just like us.

After the cheering died down, I got a sudden brainwave and whispered my idea to Surja-da. He smiled and agreed. So I went to the VIG, and handing back the trophy said, in my best, most-polite voice, 'Sir, if you please. May I return this trophy, and ask for another prize?'

The VIG's plump cheeks trembled as he nodded his head.

'Will you please allow my friend here to live in the stadium and play and learn and practise cricket?' The cricketer ghost had appeared by my side during the speech. There was a look of great hope on his face, and I sent up a quick prayer for the VIG to agree to my request.

The VIG's cheeks wobbled some more as he nodded yet again. He would allow the cricketer to stay here! Surja-da and I exchanged delighted smiles. The cricketer looked around happily. This was just the place for him.

A park by day where he could sleep in the big trees, and a stadium at night, where he could practise and perhaps become the next great ghost cricket star.

It was time for us to go. One more ghost had found his forever home. We quickly said our goodbyes and started walking back to the road. I had quite forgotten the silent sad ghost who had not flown out of the car when it had parked. Now I had to go back to her. As we walked away, I looked back.

The stadium was slowly getting blurred like it was being wiped off. Looking there now, no one would guess there had been an exciting game going on just minutes back.

Our taxi was waiting for us by the roadside. Inside it, there was the lady who had not said a word all night.

Where would I take her?

I had zilch ideas.

15

We sat in the taxi in complete silence. I could feel the minutes ticking away. I was sure we were getting closer and closer to the end of the night. If I did not get a place for the last ghost by then, she would wander homeless in this huge city, scaring herself and others. But I was completely out of ideas, and she was sitting still as stone. Surja-da cleared his throat slightly. I drummed my fingers on the dashboard of the taxi. The car, too, was quiet, which was unusual.

I had to do something. I sat up straighter and turned back in my seat to face her.

How should I address her? Ma'am? Miss? Aunty? Now that I got a better look at her, I saw that she was much frailer than the other ghosts, made of more air it seemed.

Her edges kept disappearing and reappearing. It was impossible to make out her age from seeing her.

I decided Miss would be a good way to address her.

'Miss, hello,' I started.

Her eyes slowly turned to look at me. As I looked, I felt that I too was becoming still as stone. There was something very quiet and peaceful about her eyes. After the madness of the cricket match, I suddenly wanted to just sit there with her, not speaking, not doing anything.

I shook myself. No! Not doing anything is not an option for adventurers with such big responsibilities!

Surja-da and I exchanged glances. The taxi shook, telling us to get a move on. Her eyes looked away from mine and turned to something on my lap.

I looked down and saw the little bag I had with me all night. The one in which Mama had put the torch. And the note. The note! He said I should check it if I needed help.

I *did* need help. Desperately hoping that the earlier gibberish I had read on it would make more sense now, I scrabbled around in the bag till I found it. Drawing it out, I switched on the torch and read:

Cemetery
Old tree in park

Howrah Bridge
Old well
To return, shout out 12 times table.
For any other assistance, look within.

It did make some kind of sense. Clearly, these were all the possible places to find homes for my charges. I had taken them to the cemetery, and the park. So now, should it be Howrah Bridge or old well? Might as well ask her.

'Miss,' I waved the note at her and asked, 'do you like wells or bridges?'

For some time, she said nothing. Then from somewhere, I was not sure if it was the wind or someone wailing, a tuneful moan rose all around us. I had never heard anything like it. Goosebumps ran up and down my arms. My neck prickled. It was the saddest yet most beautiful sound I had ever heard. It reminded me of the beat of the dhak during Durga Puja, and the sound of the conches. It was like the southerly wind whooshing in after a long hot day, bringing rain and relief with it. It was like Ma humming away as she dusted and rearranged the books in the shelves of her room. It was her sad face when she held the photo of my father. It made me happy. It also made me want to cry.

I blinked away the tears that were fast rising. Really, this was no time to get poetic! Did Tintin ever stop and cry? No!

I peered at the ghost. Her lips were not moving and she had that same fixed look, but the sound was definitely coming from her. Was this how she chose to speak? Why had I assumed that all ghosts would communicate the same way? How silly of me!

But what was she trying to say? Surja-da looked as clueless as me. I gingerly held out the note once more and read from it: 'Old well ...' The moan was low. 'Howrah Bridge ...' The moan rose a pitch and became more tuneful.

Yes! She wanted to go to the bridge. The taxi had caught on, and its lights had started blinking once more cheerfully.

'Istitshan Howrah BBD Bagh Chingrighata ...' it reeled off happily.

I patted the steering wheel encouragingly. 'To Howrah Bridge!'

With a jolt the taxi took off. All around us it was still dark. Nervously I checked the sky for any signs of light and crossed my fingers. I hoped we were safe. There must surely still be a couple of hours to go till daybreak, and we were not too far from Howrah Bridge.

Wait, but where on the bridge? It was a long structure made of steel, and spanned the Hooghly River. Cars rushed on it all day and night. Below it the river flowed sluggishly, filled with boats and steamers. I had seen the steel girders shining so many times in my life. Where on earth would I lodge a tuneful ghost in that place amidst all the din? I had no idea, but when I stole a glance at her, I saw that her eyes had got a slight sparkle in them, almost as if she was excited.

Oh well, I guess we would know soon.

The taxi trundled along, giving little squeaks and yelps as it went. There was an air of excitement in the car. We were about to find our last home!

As we went down a road, in the distance I could see the lines of the bridge rising up into the sky. Ma had once said the bridge was 'iconic'. I am not sure what she meant. But it always made my heart beat a bit faster, seeing it.

There was no more time to think. We were going faster and faster, picking up speed on the empty road. Usually, these roads were packed with cars and people and handcarts and rickshaws, everyone shouting and honking and sweating. Now they were quiet, inviting us to reach Howrah Bridge fast.

And then, right ahead, a row of people. A line across the road.

My heart sank. Was this another wall of angry ghosts? Or were these some other people, here for some other purpose? Was I going to have to think of yet another way to make a ghost accepted by those living there already?

The taxi came to a halt, its brakes squealing. The headlight dimmed. And in the night air, the spectacle I saw made my jaw drop.

What I had thought was one row of people was not that at all. There was a sea of people in front of me, all in neat lines. In their hands they held garlands—made of all kinds of dead flowers. They were smiling and bobbing up and down on their toes, as though they could not wait to greet us. I caught a glimpse of the river below; rows and rows of boats were floating on the water, filled with more people.

They were not people. They were many, many ghosts. Why had they gathered here in such large numbers?

There was only one way to find out. I opened the door and stepped out. At that, a happy gasp rose from everyone. Was all this for me? What had I done this time?

But no, their eyes were trained behind me, on the car. Surja-da came out of a window and reached a hand in. Miss held his hand. Then she whooshed out as well.

An excited babble rose up from the crowd.

They were not here for me. It was all for her. For Miss. The silent enigmatic ghost who had not said a word all through this exciting night.

They were all waiting for her.

16

Surja-da and I stood on either side of Miss. She raised a hand as though to wave, and then dropped it shyly to her side. Surja-da looked as clueless as me. All night he had been guiding me through the mysterious world of Kolkata's ghosts, telling me rules and little secrets. But this seemed to have puzzled him too.

I had expected the rows of ghosts to rush up and greet her. But no one did. Indeed, no one moved at all. They just gazed at her, almost unbelievingly. An awkward silence arose.

Finally, one of them stepped up. He was dressed quite nicely in traditional Bengali clothes—a dhuti and kurta with a pair of grand chappals on his feet with a front that rose up like a boat. It made funny creaky sounds as he walked up. The ghost wobbled a bit and then coming up to us, did a namaskar and bowed almost to his waist.

I shuffled my feet. Was I supposed to do namaskar back? Miss was just standing there. Her face appeared the same, but I was sure I sensed happiness around her that had been missing all night.

As the ghost straightened up, I gaped at his face. He had the biggest moustache I had ever seen—on man or ghost. The whiskers were long and thick and reached down to his waist. The lower parts were plaited and bows made of ribbons twirled off the ends. I had really seen nothing like them before—and tonight I had seen plenty of new things.

I tore my eyes away from them and tried to listen to what he was saying. For such a large and regal person, he was speaking in a very low tone. But Miss could hear him perfectly, I guessed, because she gave a small smile. Seeing her smile made my heart lift in happiness. There was something about the way she looked now—beautiful and serene—that made me want to make her keep smiling.

But first, I had to hear what on earth they were saying. What a change after the screaming cricket spectators! No one was jumping up and down here. No one was waving banners. In fact, there was only an air of quiet all around.

Finally, I could catch a word or two: 'River … song … honour … legend.'

I turned again to Surja-da for some help. He seemed to have caught on to what was happening, because he was smiling gently too. He leaned across to me and said, 'Famous singer.'

Ah, so Miss was a famous ghost singer! Looking at the grand welcome laid out for her, I supposed she was the Queen of Melody in this world. But how had they known she would come here today? Did she not just make up her mind?

I listened in closely to the welcoming ghost's words, straining my ears. Really, I wished these ghosts would mumble less and speak more clearly. He seemed to be saying a whole speech all in a whisper.

'Word reached … Queen … airwaves … so came … waves in river … delight and honour … live here … river … forever.'

Surja-da stepped in with the explanation. 'They heard through their radio channels that she was in the city. They all gathered here because she comes from a river.'

That made sense. Mama had told me that many of the ghosts had to move away when the places they lived in became unliveable for them. Perhaps Miss had been staying in the waters of a river somewhere in the countryside. Something must have happened to the river to make her leave. Perhaps it had become too polluted, or the water had become less. I remember Ma telling me how rivers changed course, sometimes taking new routes. For whatever reason, the star of the ghost singing world had taken the train to Sealdah station and come to Kolkata. And then she had ridden around in the taxi with us all night, hoping to find a place where she could stay and sing once more in peace.

And we had found it! There was a large river here—the Hooghly. It wasn't very quiet usually, but the ghosts who had come here all looked happy enough.

Now another ghost stepped forward and mumbled something. Whatever she said made Miss look almost excited. The second ghost placed a garland of dead roses around Miss's neck. She held out another one for me and I shrank back a bit from the musty smell. But since it would be rude not to, I accepted it. Surja-da was wearing a garland of withered marigolds now.

What next? No one seemed to be in a hurry. In fact, everyone was very polite and just nodded at one another. The neat rows of people in front of us were also quiet.

I had never seen so many people be so quiet together. It was like our school principal's dream come true.

Finally, I felt I had to do something, so I said, 'Miss will live with you here now.'

I had spoken in my usual voice, but in this silent crowd it sounded like I had shouted into a megaphone. Embarrassed, I shut my mouth. But the crowd was good-natured. I guessed they had gotten used to loud sounds after living around the noisy bridge.

'Yes,' the first ghost whispered. 'But first, a welcome concert.'

Out of nowhere, a few seats appeared for us. They were large fancy chairs, like the ones you would see in old homes. I sat gingerly on one. Surja-da and Miss took the others.

The music started. I could not make out what the instruments were. Surely they were not ones I knew, because the music was a mix of what would come from a sitar, a flute, and a tabla all put together. The opening strains were slow, but gradually it increased in volume and tempo. And then the voices joined in.

I had never heard a sound like it. The music seemed to enter my heart directly without going into my ears. The notes spread themselves out all over me. Some parts of me felt sad. But my hands beat a rhythm on their own. My feet moved gradually up and down. And then, from nowhere, a huge wave washed over me.

It was not water from the Hooghly—thank God. I did not fancy getting a dunking in the river. This was a wave of pure emotions. All the love I felt for Ma, all the excitement of going on an adventure, that feeling of happiness when I open a new book, the sadness when I think of my absent Baba—all of it came together at once with the song and the music.

All I wanted to do now was to sit there and go on listening.

The voices ...

The strains of unearthly music ...

The cool wind from the river ...

The gentle lapping of the waves somewhere ...

My eyes were closing ... closing ... closing ... Now they were shut tight. Some tears leaked out. They fell and tickled my nose and ears. But I didn't want to wipe them away.

17

'Cawww!'

I trembled in my sleep.

'Kaaa kaaa kaaa …'

Where was I? Were the crows calling already? A hard beak was pecking away at me. I swiped at it angrily in my sleep. How annoying! After all that music to be woken by a rude crow! I would not allow it. I would sleep some more.

But now the crow was shaking me awake. Really! This was too much.

I opened one eye. It made no sense. So I slowly opened the other.

The night was still dark overhead, but a few crows had started wheeling above. One of them had hopped close to me and was staring at me with beady eyes.

'Shoo!' I sent it on its way and it hopped off in a dignified manner.

I looked around. Gone were the singers. Gone, the boats filled with ghosts. There was absolutely no one around me. Only the metal beams of Howrah Bridge rising up into the dark—white and solid. I was lying by the side of the road. Someone had thoughtfully placed a pillow under my head and covered me with a soft kantha blanket. I gathered these up and looked for the taxi. And where was Surja-da? Surely he would not vanish and leave me?

He hadn't. He was standing on the bridge, looking into the waters below. I joined him.

'Surja-da, we did it! Everyone has a home now.'

'Home,' he repeated softly. I felt a sudden wish to hug him. I guessed that was not possible. But in my mind I put him down as the kindest ghost of all.

'Where's the taxi?' I asked. We needed to get back to Sealdah station and meet up with Mama and the Leader, and report all that had happened.

Surja-da shrugged. The taxi was gone. I felt sad at losing our talkative friend. I guess it had found other passengers. Kolkata taxis are notorious that way, Ma said.

'How will we get back now?' I wondered.

Surja-da's eyes glittered as he looked away from the water and at me.

'Tables,' he said.

Huh? Tables would take us back? How? And from where would we get tables now? Even the chairs were gone!

'Tables?' I asked again. 'How many?'

'Twelve.'

And then it came back to me. That note! 'Shout out 12 times table.'

I knew my tables well! And 12 times was the easiest after the 10s.

'Surja-da! Let's go! I want to see Mama and the Leader and all our friends, they will be back now too!'

Surja-da nodded happily. We held hands. I had no idea what would happen once I said the tables, but here it went …

'12 oneza 12!' we said together.

We were lifted a few inches off the road. I could not believe it. We were actually floating. *I* was floating, like I had seen the ghosts do all night!

We nodded to each other again, grinning.

'12 twoza 24!'

'12 threeza 36!'

With every multiple we rose higher and higher. By 60 we were floating well above the road. By 84 we were flying!

On and on we chanted the tables and on and on we flew. I was not scared at all. Instead, I felt delighted. From high above, I saw the whole city. The lights were now twinkling brighter, like the magic mist that had made everything dull had been lifted. Here and there, a few people were walking around. Some were jogging, some others were clanking their milk vessels. Even from up here I could see it all clearly.

'12 thirteenza 156!'

I was astonished I knew the tables so well but I didn't want to stop to think and perhaps crash land into a milk cart below.

In no time the signs of Sealdah station started coming up. We were nearly there!

'12 twentyza 240!' we yelled triumphantly as the station loomed up ahead.

We stopped saying the tables. But we didn't crash. We gently wafted down as if we had parachutes strapped on. Like feathers in the wind—well, Surja-da was mostly wind—he and I landed at the entrance to the station. I wondered if it was still the ghost station of the night before or a regular one again. Where would I find everyone?

I needn't have worried. Mama was standing there, hands on his hips, scanning the skies for us. He was wearing his normal clothes again.

'Mama!' I called out to him.

'Poltu!' he ran up. 'You are back,' he added somewhat unnecessarily.

'I found homes for them all, Mama,' I said to him in excitement. 'And I saw a tea party, and a cricket match, and a concert. And I was Sudden Not Death.'

'You don't say,' Mama grabbed my hand and pulled me close. Only now I realized he must have been worried

about me. I quailed to think what Ma would have to say to him—and me—if she heard what we had been doing all night.

'What now, Mama?' I asked.

'Now? The train is nearly here. A good eight hours late. So we can take it and go to Jalpaiguri as planned.'

The thought of an ordinary holiday seemed quite nice to me. It would be good to be around people who could not detach their own heads or fly around like balloons. But what about all my new friends? Surja-da? Leader? All the others? Taxiji?

Surja-da was hugging me. Well, not exactly hugging, but enveloping me in a mist. And behind him I could see Khepa, Lalmoni, and Bhola, waiting to give more hugs and to shake my hand. Even the Leader was there, a signboard where her head should be that said, 'Goodbye c u'. And Taxiji had reappeared too, its headlights flashing cheerfully.

'Well done, bnoy,' Khepa cheered. Lalmoni winked, and Bhola popped in a green Gems from a packet in Mama's hand. I wanted to hear all about their adventures of the night, but the train would leave any minute now.

I blinked back my tears. Had they been friends only for one night?

Mama looked down at me and grinned. 'Don't cry, Poltu. They will be here when we come back. And once a Ghost Traffic Warden, always a Ghost Traffic Warden … Now, quick! Here's your bag. Let's catch our train.'

We hurried away to the platform. The station was just as it always was, with porters running up and down, trains huffing in, people hurrying to catch their trains, the station announcements making no sense at all to my ears.

We found our train and jumped in. As we reached our seats, it started to pull away from the platform. I leaned out of the window. Among all the hustle and bustle I tried to see the ghosts. All I saw were ordinary humans.

Then I spotted some benches with figures sleeping on them. Covered in blankets.

Now I knew who they were.

They were my friends and my partners in the best adventure ever. We would surely have many more.

I waved at the sleeping figures. I would be back soon.

Acknowledgements

After years of being on the other side of the bookmaking process, it took a leap of faith to tell this story that arrived in my head one sleepy afternoon. It's incredible how many it takes to make a book, and I will always be privileged to intimately know this puzzle that is the publishing world.

My heartfelt thanks to:

My agent Kanishka Gupta for his immediate and unflagging enthusiasm about the book.

Publisher Tina Narang for liking this story enough to want to publish it.

My editor Aparna Kapur for her detailed edits and valuable suggestions; Nimmy Chacko for ironing out the wrinkles with her sharp copyedits; and Ankita Deshpande for her attentive proofreading. Editors WILL save the world!

The brilliant illustrator Pankaj Saikia who plucked these characters from my head and brought them to life with his joyful artwork.

Friends and first readers to whom I could work up the courage to show this when it was a manuscript:

Bijal Vachharajani, whose astute comments added much to the story and who has not ceased to be amused at my attempts at being the perfect writer person.

Radhika Sathe Mantri, whose verdict I awaited nervously while she read the draft, and who helped co-create the wonderful space where much of this book got written—Cosy Nook Library.

Ravi Singh, who heard the outline of the story over pork chops in Delhi's Nagaland Kitchen and gave me the courage to go ahead with the writing.

My family, Ma, Baba and Didibhai, Maitreyi, Subid and Tilottama Shome, each one a unique kind of storyteller, who gave me a childhood I can look back on today and see the fun and happiness.

Ma and Baba, Bandana and Subir Ghosh, who have for years and years told me to get down and write.

My forever companion and husband Arnab, patient listener, fount of common sense, best friend.

And finally Ishaan (Opu), who brings joy wherever he goes and would even help needy ghosts if required, much like Poltu.

About the Author

Sudeshna Shome Ghosh is a reader, writer, and editor of books for children and adults. When she is not reading a book, or worrying about which book to read next, she works as an editor. In fact, she has worked in the Indian publishing industry for over 25 years. She is also co-founder of Cosy Nook Library, a children's library in Bangalore. She has written and translated books for children and published a number of articles and book reviews in various publications. She can usually be found in her home in Bangalore lounging on her couch, reading, dozing, or drinking tea.

About the Illustrator

Pankaj Saikia is an illustrator and children's book author hailing from the state of Assam. As an illustrator, he is primarily focused on specializing in picture books and graphic novels. He has authored two picture books and has illustrated many others. His wordless picture book *Theatre of Ghosts* was listed in the prestigious Parag Honour List 2023.

HarperCollins *Publishers* India

At HarperCollins India, we believe in telling the best stories and finding the widest readership for our books in every format possible. We started publishing in 1992; a great deal has changed since then, but what has remained constant is the passion with which our authors write their books, the love with which readers receive them, and the sheer joy and excitement that we as publishers feel in being a part of the publishing process.

Over the years, we've had the pleasure of publishing some of the finest writing from the subcontinent and around the world, including several award-winning titles and some of the biggest bestsellers in India's publishing history. But nothing has meant more to us than the fact that millions of people have read the books we published, and that somewhere, a book of ours might have made a difference.

As we look to the future, we go back to that one word—a word which has been a driving force for us all these years.

Read.